USBORNE

LEARN TO PLAY
BEETHOVEN

Michael Durnin
Emma Danes

Designed by Julia Rheam
Illustrated by Peter Dennis

Music arrangements by Daniel Scott

Series editor: Anthony Marks

Contents

Beethoven's early life	4
Sonatina	6
Octet, op.103	8
Mollys Abschied, op.52 no.5	10
Sextet, op.81	12
Beethoven and his age	14
Piano concerto no.1, op.15	16
Ah! Perfido, op.65	18
Quintet, op.16	20
Bagatelle, op.33 no.6	21
Scherzo, op.9 no.2	22
Success in Vienna	24
Kreutzer Sonata, op.47	26
Variations on "God save the King"	28
Eroica Symphony, op.55	30
Razumovsky Quartet, op.59 no.2	32
Variations	34
The symphony	35
Violin concerto, op.61	36
Symphony no.5, op.67	37
Pastoral Symphony, op.68	38
Für Elise	40
Harp Quartet, op.74	41
Beethoven's final years	42
Archduke Trio, op.97	44
Symphony no.7, op.92	46
An die ferne Geliebte, op.98	47
Pianos	48
The orchestra	49
Symphony no.8, op.93	50
Violin sonata, op.96	52
Fidelio, op.72	54
Bagatelle, op.126 no.5	56
Symphony no.9, op.125	58
String quartet, op.130	59
Playing the pieces	60
Important dates in Beethoven's life	62
Glossary	63
Index	64

Beethoven is one of the most important composers in the history of music. This book contains more than 25 of his pieces, arranged for piano or electronic keyboard, and simplified to make them easier to play. Most of them are extracts from longer pieces that were originally written for the piano, orchestra or other combinations of instruments and voices. They appear in the book in roughly the order that Beethoven wrote them.

Most of the pieces are arranged for one person to play. But some you can play either on your own or with a friend, and one is for two players on one piano. For more about this, and hints about how to play each piece, see the section called "Playing the pieces" on pages 60-61. On page 62 there is a list of the most important events in Beethoven's life. Musical terms and other unfamiliar words are explained in the glossary on page 63.

Beethoven gave his pieces opus numbers as they were published (opus is the Latin word for "work" or "piece"; it is often shortened to "op."). Some early pieces have high opus numbers because they were not published until many years after Beethoven wrote them. In this book, the opus numbers are given after the titles of the pieces. A few pieces have no opus numbers because they were not published during Beethoven's lifetime. They were found and published after his death.

Some of Beethoven's music was published under the name Louis van Beethoven. Louis is the French version of Ludwig.

Nobody knows the exact date on which Ludwig van Beethoven was born. He was baptised in the German town of Bonn on December 17, 1770. This means he was probably born a few days before that. But Beethoven himself was confused about his birth date later in his life. He believed that he was up to two years younger than he really was.

The house in Bonn where Beethoven was born

Beethoven had two younger brothers, Caspar and Nikolaus. Both his father, Johann, and his grandfather, also called Ludwig, were musicians. They worked at the court of the Elector of Cologne, an important prince in Bonn. Johann was not a very successful musician. He also drank heavily, and behaved badly to his wife, Maria Magdalena, and to his children. But Ludwig was very important at the court. Beethoven was only three years old when Ludwig died, but he admired his grandfather throughout his life, and tried hard to match his success.

Portrait of Ludwig, Beethoven's grandfather

Early musical studies

Beethoven aged sixteen

At first, Beethoven was taught piano and violin by his father. Between the ages of 10 and 22 he studied with Christian Gottlob Neefe, the court organist at Bonn. Neefe recognized Beethoven's talent and encouraged him as a musician. He found Beethoven a post at the court when he was only 12 years old, and arranged for some of his compositions to be published. The first of these, *Nine Variations on a March by Dressler*, was published in 1782. In his early teens, Beethoven wrote lots of music, including a piano concerto, three piano sonatas and three quartets for piano and strings.

But in 1785 he almost stopped composing for about four years. During this period he visited Vienna in Austria, one of the greatest musical cities of the

Title page of the first edition of Beethoven's Dressler Variations

time. He was probably sent by the Elector of Cologne, who wanted the musicians there to judge his abilities. One of the people Beethoven met in Vienna was the famous composer and pianist Wolfgang Amadeus Mozart. Mozart recognized immediately that Beethoven was a brilliant musician.

Beethoven wanted to stay in Vienna to study with Mozart. But after only two weeks he was forced to return to Bonn because his mother became seriously ill. She died on July 17, 1787. Johann was extremely distressed by his wife's death, and became unable to look after the family. He left his post at the Elector's court, and moved with his children to a small village outside Bonn.

As the eldest son, Beethoven had to take responsibility for the running of the family and household. From November 1789, the Elector of Cologne arranged for half of Johann's salary to be paid to Beethoven. During this period, Beethoven had little time to compose, but he made some money by giving concerts and recitals.

Bonn in the late 18th century

Further education

In 1789, Beethoven enrolled at Bonn University. He became very interested in politics and literature, and the philosophy and learning of his day (there is more about this on pages 14-15). At about this time he also began to compose again, trying pieces for many combinations of instruments and voices. He composed cantatas (works for choir and orchestra), ballet scores, piano variations, trios, wind pieces and songs.

A page of exercises from one of Beethoven's study books

In 1792, Beethoven met Joseph Haydn, one of the most famous and successful composers of the day. He showed Haydn some of his work, probably at Neefe's suggestion. Haydn was impressed, and agreed to teach him. In November, Beethoven went to Vienna to begin his studies. Soon after he arrived there, he received the news that his father had died. He never returned to Bonn.

Joseph Haydn

In Vienna, Beethoven studied with various important composers as well as Haydn. These included Johann Schenk, Johann Georg Albrechtsberger and Antonio Salieri.

Success in Vienna

Beethoven's career flourished from the moment when he arrived in Vienna. Although he was still thought of as a student composer, he was

Miniature of Beethoven as a young man

very successful as a performer. His energetic and exciting playing made him one of the most popular pianists of the day. He went on tours to Prague, Dresden, Leipzig and Berlin, playing at royal courts and in public concerts.

From about 1795, Beethoven's reputation as a composer also spread quickly. His music was published and sold throughout Europe. He wrote to his brother Nikolaus that he was winning friends, fame and money. Most of the friends that Beethoven made at this time were wealthy aristocrats. Several of them supported Beethoven financially, and helped him in his career. Beethoven dedicated his first

symphony to Baron van Swieten, who was one of his strongest supporters. Swieten had also been friends with the composers Mozart and Haydn.

Beethoven also played the viola.

Prince Karl Lichnowsky, one of the most important patrons in Europe, also supported Beethoven. In return, Beethoven dedicated several pieces to him, including his Pathétique Sonata and his second symphony.

TROIS TRIOS
Pour le Piano Forte

CHARLES ⋅ LICHNOWSKY

LOUIS van BEETHOVEN

Title page of three piano trios dedicated to Lichnowsky

Lichnowsky helped to spread Beethoven's fame to all the aristocracy of Europe. He was also one of Beethoven's closest friends. Beethoven often stayed with him at one of his palaces.

During this time, many people seemed to think that Beethoven himself was an aristocrat. Beethoven did not reveal the truth about his background until 1818.

A square in Vienna where Beethoven lived

5

Sonatina

A sonatina is a fairly short and often light-hearted piece. Sonatinas were very popular in the late 18th century and early 19th century.

This piece was not published in Beethoven's lifetime, but experts are fairly sure that he wrote it. It was found with his other papers when he died.

The sign ♩ = 112 at the start of this piece is a metronome mark. A metronome is a machine that ticks steadily. On the right are some early ticking machines.

In this piece, set a metronome to tick 112 beats each minute. This tells you how fast to play. You can find out about Beethoven's metronome on page 51.

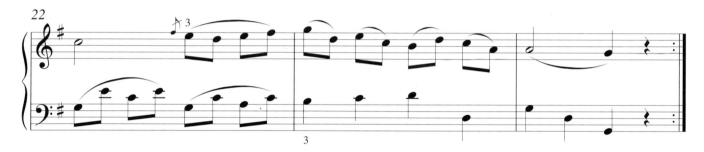

Octet, op.103 (part B)

This music is arranged for two players at one piano. The person on the right plays Part A. Duet arrangements were also very popular in Beethoven's time.

Beethoven wrote this piece in 1792, just before leaving Bonn for Vienna. His friends gave him an album of drawings and verses as a farewell present (see left).

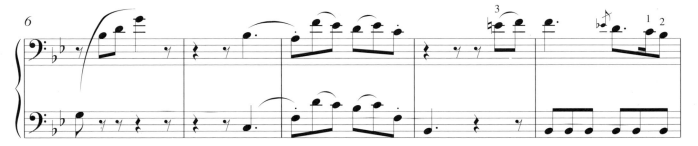

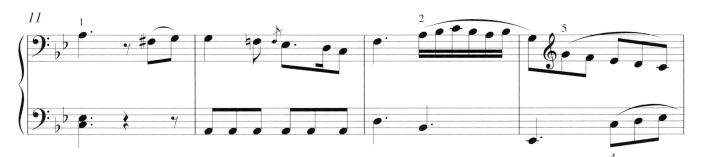

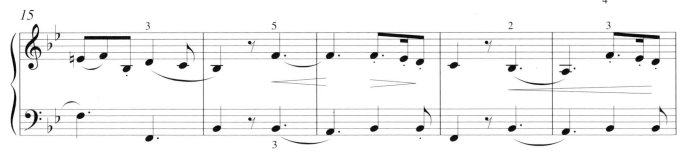

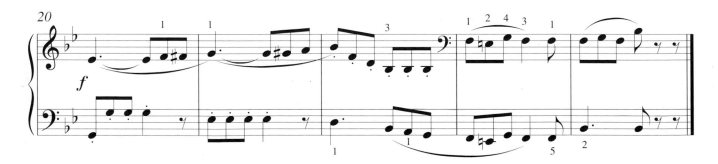

Octet, op.103 (part A)

An octet is a piece for eight musicians, each playing a different part. This one is for two oboes, two clarinets, two bassoons and two horns.

Beethoven wrote this octet for his employer, Maximilian Franz (shown left). Music for wind groups was very popular in Germany in the 18th century.

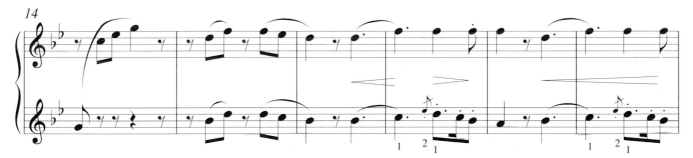

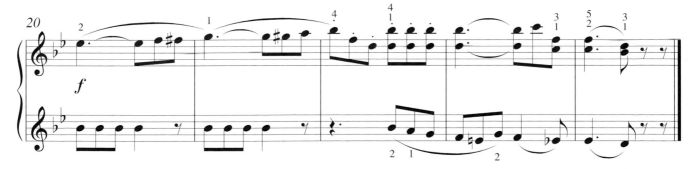

Mollys Abschied, op.52 no.5

The title of this song means "Molly's farewell". Beethoven wrote over 80 songs in all. They are the first examples of a German song-style called *lieder*.

In lieder, the music matches the mood of the words very closely. Franz Schubert (shown left), who knew Beethoven, was the greatest composer of lieder.

Beethoven's sketchbooks

Beethoven probably made more pages of musical jottings and sketches than any other composer of his time. He filed them carefully so he could refer back to them later for ideas. Several thousand pages of sketches still exist. Some are in large volumes, some in small, portable notepads, others on loose sheets of paper. Some of the sketches are only tiny fragments of tunes and rhythms, many of which were never used. Others are detailed workings of whole pieces or movements, sometimes on several staves.

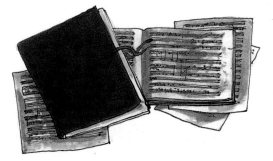

Play the bottom two lines on the piano. The top line is the singer's part. You could ask a friend to play it on a flute, recorder or violin, while you play the piano.

In most lieder, the singer's part is very similar to the top line of the piano. You can hear this if you play this piece with a friend, or hum the top line as you play.

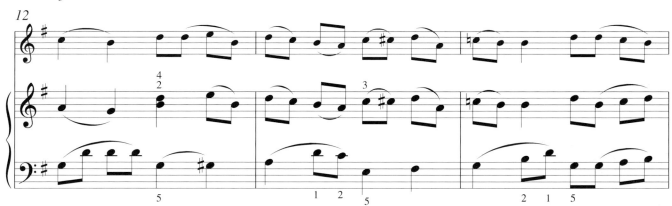

Many experts have studied Beethoven's sketches, to see how they developed into pieces. But it is sometimes very difficult to decide which piece a sketch was for. Beethoven used the sketches mainly as reminders, leaving gaps where he did not need to fill everything in. He often left out clefs, accidentals and key signatures. Even the notes are sometimes unclear. Some of the more detailed and complicated sketches are for pieces he never completed. The sketch on the left was for a tenth symphony. It was the last page of music he wrote.

Sextet, op.81

A sextet is a piece of chamber music for a combination of six solo instruments. You can find out more about chamber music at the bottom of the page.

Beethoven wrote this sextet for an unusual combination: two violins, one viola, one cello and two horns. This tune is from the last movement (section).

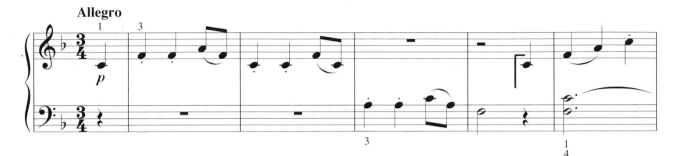

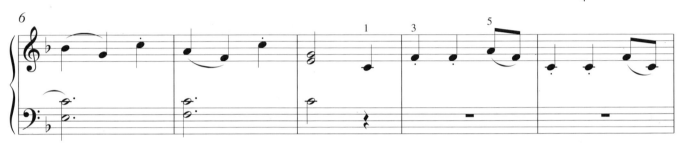

Chamber music

Chamber music is for small groups of players, usually no more than eight, each playing a separate line of music. It is intended to be played in large rooms, like the one shown here, not concert halls. The audience sits close to the musicians. There is usually no conductor. The players decide together how to interpret the music, and watch and listen to each other as they play.

Beethoven probably wrote this piece in about 1795, the year in which he gave his first public concert in Vienna. But it was not published until 1810.

The horn part uses a small range of notes. This is because to play other notes, the player had to add or remove sections of tube. This was hard to do quickly.

Chamber music was very popular in Beethoven's time. Many wealthy patrons employed resident chamber music groups and held concerts in their homes. Beethoven wrote a great deal of chamber music, for many combinations of instruments, with and without piano. In this book you can play parts of two quartets, a quintet, a sextet and an octet. Beethoven also wrote several trios and a septet.

Beethoven directing a quintet

Beethoven was very influenced by the work of earlier composers, mainly those of the previous century, and especially J. S. Bach. But he developed many new ways of writing music, and his lifestyle and interests also changed the way later composers lived and worked.

An arrangement by Beethoven of a piece by Bach

Unlike most 18th century composers, Beethoven used his music to express non-musical ideas. For example, in the Pastoral Symphony he tried to convey the wildness and calm of nature. He based other pieces on political ideas, for example *Fidelio* (see page 54), *Egmont* (music for a tragic play) and the final choral movement of his ninth symphony (see page 58).

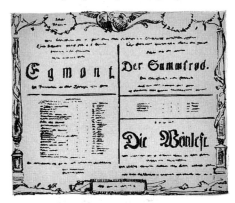

Schedule for a performance of *Egmont*

In this way, Beethoven greatly expanded people's ideas about what music could express.

Beethoven also developed a new way of writing music which influenced many later composers. In the middle of the 18th century, most composers had been writing music which consisted of a single tune with a fairly simple accompaniment. Composers such as Haydn and Mozart wrote in this style, although they tried to make

Interior of a music store in Vienna

their accompaniments more interesting. But Beethoven experimented with writing much more complicated music. In this, he was influenced by the dense and intricate music written much earlier by composers such as J. S. Bach.

Audience at the first performance of the seventh symphony

The Eroica Symphony and the Hammerklavier Sonata are both written in this new style.

Beethoven also changed the way composers were thought of. He was the first composer who was financially independent, and the first who made a huge impact on the general public.

A concert hall in the Augarten, Vienna

In the late 18th century, more people started to go to concerts. Beethoven's recitals, and performances of his music, made him very famous in Vienna.

Romanticism

In the 18th century, advances in science and philosophy influenced almost every area of people's lives. New scientific values of order, clarity and reason affected ideas about art and politics. The growth of industry encouraged more and more people to move from the country to live in the towns and cities.

But not everybody shared this confidence in reason, thought and industry. Many writers, painters and musicians,

A bust of Beethoven

including Beethoven, believed that instinct and feeling were just as important. They reacted against the ugliness of towns and cities, and were fascinated by nature's wildness and power. They were part of a trend known today as Romanticism.

Many Romantics also thought of life as a struggle, which the heroic individual had to fight. Beethoven agreed with this, and always set himself obstacles which he could struggle against while he was composing.

Romantic paintings often expressed the power of nature

Politics

During the late 18th century, many people in different parts of the world began to question the authority and wealth of their leaders. In France, people began openly to oppose the authorities. They hoped to establish a more democratic system, based on the ideas of liberty, equality and brotherhood. The years of fighting which followed became known as the French Revolution.

The storming of the Bastille

However, the Revolution quickly became brutal and violent. The king and queen were arrested, out of hatred for their luxurious lifestyle. Fearing revolution in their own countries, Austria and Prussia joined forces to invade France. The French troops which defeated them were led by a young general, Napoleon Bonaparte. The king and queen were executed, and a bitter struggle for the control of France followed.

Outside France, many people, including Beethoven, greatly admired Napoleon. He appeared to be a great Romantic hero, struggling to speak out for the freedom of the people. Many rulers in other countries, however, were increasingly afraid of revolution, and became more and more oppressive. Beethoven spoke out very strongly against the Viennese authorities for denying their people liberty.

However, Napoleon became very ambitious for his own glory, and Beethoven soon became very disillusioned with him. In 1804 Napoleon declared himself Emperor of France, and for ten years fought to conquer Europe and North Africa. He invaded Austria, and occupied Vienna twice.

Wellington

In 1813, Beethoven wrote a piece called *Wellington's Victory*, to celebrate Napoleon's defeat in Spain by the English army leader, Wellington. In 1814, when Napoleon was finally defeated, he wrote a cantata called *The Glorious Moment*. In the general celebrations, his opera *Fidelio* was performed more than 20 times, with great success.

A poster with the revolution message of liberty, equality and fraternity

Beethoven approved of the motives of the Revolution. In 1789, French rioters stormed the Bastille prison in Paris to free the prisoners. Although there were few prisoners there, the attack became a symbol of the power of the people against authority.

Napoleon as a young man

Napoleon's army invading Vienna

Title page of *Wellington's Victory*

But although Beethoven believed in freedom and equality, he himself never particularly condemned the aristocracy. He was willing to flatter them when he needed their financial support to help him make a living.

Piano concerto no.1, op.15

Beethoven wrote this piano concerto in 1795. He dedicated it to one of his piano pupils, Countess Babette Keglevics (shown on the right).

Beethoven himself gave the first performance of this piece. This was in a concert given by Haydn shortly after Beethoven arrived in Vienna.

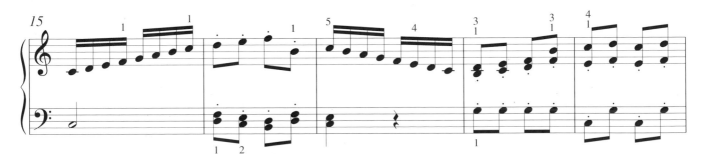

Concertos

A concerto is a piece for one or more soloists, accompanied by an orchestra. The soloist is usually the star of the piece, playing much more difficult and exciting music than the musicians in the orchestra.

Beethoven wrote only seven

concertos. Five were for the piano, the instrument he liked most, one was for violin, and one was for a trio of piano, violin and cello. This was far fewer than Mozart, but Beethoven's concertos were very different from any previous ones.

This movement is a rondo. In a rondo, the main tune keeps returning, with other music in between. Beethoven finished it two days before the concert.

But at the concert, the piano was out of tune. Beethoven had to play the piano part in a different key to make it match the music played by the orchestra.

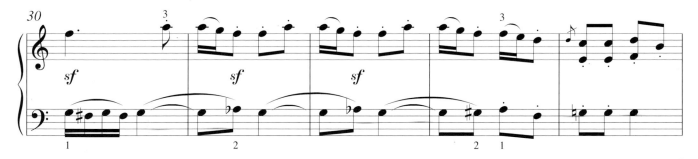

Beethoven wanted his concertos to be very dramatic. He imagined the soloist as a solitary hero, challenging a large orchestra. The soloist's music is very different from the orchestra's, as well as being much more difficult. For

A "heroic" violinist playing the solo part in a concerto

example, in Beethoven's last two piano concertos, the rhythms, tempos and phrasings in the piano solo part are much more inventive than those played by the orchestra. It is as though the pianist is making the music up while playing.

Ah! Perfido, op.65

This is an elaborate, operatic-style song, written to be performed with an orchestra. Because it is not part of an opera, it is called a concert aria.

Ask a friend to play the top line on a melody instrument, or you could hum the top line and play the bottom two. Or play the top and bottom lines on the piano.

Adagio

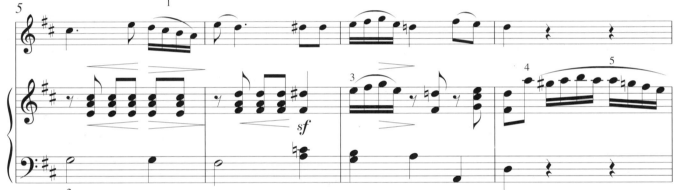

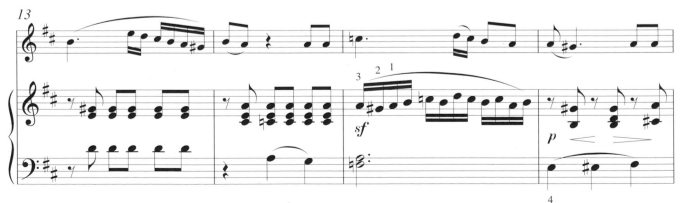

Beethoven wrote this aria for Josephine von Clary, a well-known amateur singer (shown right), although she did not give the first performance.

The words (called the libretto) were written by Metastasio, a famous Italian poet who worked in Vienna. The title means "Ah! treacherous person".

Quintet, op.16

This piece is for a piano, an oboe, a clarinet, a bassoon and a horn. At the first performance, Beethoven himself played the piano part.

Mozart wrote what he thought was his best piece for the same combination. Beethoven wrote his quintet because he admired Mozart's so much.

Andante cantabile

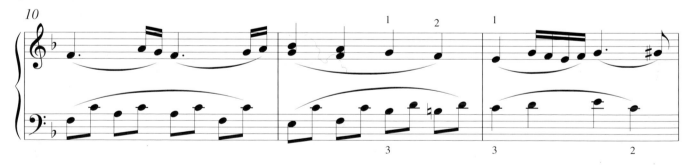

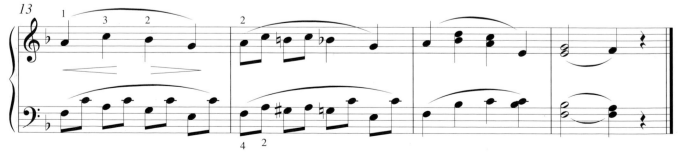

Bagatelle, op.33 no.6

A bagatelle is a short, light-hearted piece, usually played on the piano. Most bagatelles were published in sets. This one is the sixth in a set of seven.

Beethoven wrote this piece in 1802, using fragments of music rejected from piano sonatas. On the left you can see the street where he lived at about this time.

Allegretto quasi andante

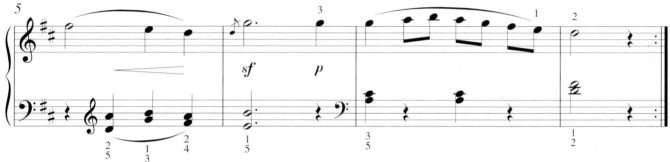

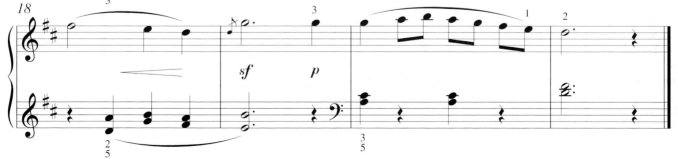

Scherzo, op.9 no.2

Scherzo means "joke" in Italian. A scherzo is a lively piece. This one is a movement from a string trio. A string trio consists of one violin, one viola and one cello.

The string trios were published in 1798 by Artaria and Co., a Viennese firm (their offices are shown left). Find out more about music publishing below.

Publishing

When composers today write a piece of original music, they are protected by the law of copyright. This means nobody else can use it for their own profit. Composers receive a fee from performers who want to play the music, and from publishers who want to publish it. They also recieve a certain amount of money for every copy of the music that is sold after it has been published.

In Beethoven's time, there was no copyright law in Vienna. Publishers only had to pay composers an initial fee.

The publisher, Domenico Artaria of Artaria and Co., with his wife, Theresa

Composers did not get any money for sales of their music, or for performances. Because of this, composers had to search for the publisher who would give them the highest initial fee for their work. There was also no international agreement on copyright. This meant Beethoven could sell the same music to different publishers in different countries. Both composers and publishers frequently cheated each other. Beethoven often promised the same work to several publishers, so he could take a fee from each of them.

The trios were dedicated to Count Browne-Camus (shown right). Once, when Beethoven dedicated a piece to him, Browne-Camus gave him a horse.

Beethoven forgot about the horse until he got a large bill for its food. His servant meanwhile had been secretly renting it out. He sold it soon after this.

Watermarks

In the 1960s, experts discovered a new way to estimate the date of Beethoven's musical sketches. This involves examining the paper he wrote on.

In Beethoven's time, most paper was hand-made. It was made in large sheets which were folded twice and cut, making four smaller sheets. During the process, the papermaker introduced a mark in the paper called a watermark. Part of the watermark usually came out on all four sheets. This means experts can fit together sheets from the same batch of paper.

Experts can estimate the dates of the batches of paper because the makers frequently changed their watermarks. Beethoven bought paper in large quantities and usually used it up before he bought any more. This means that each new batch of paper he bought was likely to have a different watermark.

Manuscript paper can be traced even more accurately because the staves were usually ruled by a machine in the shop that sold it. Each machine gave the rules slightly different, distinctive imperfections.

Beethoven was very popular in Vienna, both with the aristocracy and with public audiences. His greatest success at first was as a pianist, but he was also very ambitious as a composer. Between 1798 and 1802 he wrote piano trios, string trios, six string quartets, a third piano concerto, and sonatas for piano and violin. He also wrote his first two symphonies.

Announcement of Beethoven's first public concert, held in 1800

First hearing problems

In about 1798, Beethoven began to have difficulty hearing. His doctor told him that this was connected with other temporary illnesses. But Beethoven was very worried that any loss of hearing might affect his ability to compose music. He became moody and unsociable, and began to acquire a reputation for grumpiness. His doctor advised him to move into the country for a time so he could rest and relax.

In 1802, Beethoven went to stay in Heiligenstadt, a small village outside Vienna. But his panic increased when a friend drew his attention to a shepherd's flute playing in the distance. He could not hear it. He wrote a letter to his brothers that he never sent. It was found among his papers after he died. It is known as the Heiligenstadt Testament. In it, Beethoven tried to explain that he did not mean to be temperamental or moody, but that he could not bear the idea of going deaf.

The Heiligenstadt Testament on Beethoven's desk

In 1804, Beethoven finished his third symphony, the Eroica. It was much longer than Haydn's and Mozart's symphonies, and the most demanding piece Beethoven had ever written. In composing it, he believed that he had discovered a new way of putting music together (there is more about this on page 35).

The title page of Beethoven's Eroica Symphony

The symphony was first performed privately, at Prince Lobkowitz's palace in Vienna. Lobkowitz was one of Beethoven's patrons. Beethoven conducted the first public performance. But by this time he had trouble hearing high notes. Soon he found he could not hear the wind instruments at all.

Prince Lobkowitz

The church at Heiligenstadt

Prince Lobkowitz's palace

Beethoven's hearing got steadily worse, and by 1808 he had to give up performing. Although this was a tragedy, it meant that he had more time to develop his ideas about composing.

Continuing success

From 1804, Beethoven's music was performed as often as Mozart's and Haydn's. He was the best known composer in Europe. Around eight sets of his pieces were published each year from 1803 to 1812, in Vienna, Bonn, Leipzig and Zurich.

Many wealthy and important patrons recognized Beethoven's talents. In 1809, three of them made a contract to guarantee him enough money to live on, so long as he stayed in Vienna.

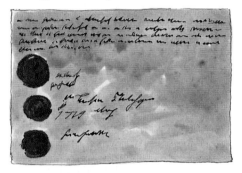

The signatures on the contract guaranteeing Beethoven an income

But Beethoven was more financially independent than any previous composer. He was so well known that piano makers gave him free pianos to get publicity. Earlier composers such as Mozart made a living by performing, publishing and teaching. But in comparison with them, Beethoven was rich. He made a lot of money just from composing and a little teaching.

Beethoven never allowed his patrons to think they could influence his music, even when, like Prince Lichnowsky, they paid him a regular allowance.

Grätz Castle, one of Prince Lichnowsky's palaces

On one occasion, Lichnowsky asked him to play in a concert. Beethoven became furious because he disapproved of the event, and in his rage he broke a statue of the prince. Later, when they were friends again, Beethoven sometimes still locked Lichnowsky out of his work room. He was the first composer who was wealthy enough to be so independent. He did not rely solely on his patrons for money, so he did not feel he had to do whatever they asked.

For example, Lichnowsky stopped paying Beethoven's allowance when they argued, so Beethoven arranged a special concert to raise money. This included the first performances of both his fifth and sixth symphonies, his fourth piano concerto, the aria *Ah! Perfido* and one movement from a mass. In this way he was able to raise the money he needed without having to rely on any of his patrons.

Beethoven aged around 45

In 1813, Beethoven's brother Caspar Carl became very ill. He died in November 1815. Before his death, Beethoven persuaded him to sign a legal document that appointed him the guardian of Caspar's son, Karl van Beethoven.

Beethoven playing a piano given to him by Conrad Graf, a Viennese piano maker

The Immortal Beloved

Beethoven never married, but he fell in love several times. In 1812 he wrote a letter to his "Immortal Beloved". It was found after his death. Nobody knows who the letter was to, or why he never sent it. Many people think it was to Antonie Brentano. She seems to

Portrait of Antonie Brentano

have been the only woman he really wanted to marry.

Kreutzer Sonata, op.47

This sonata was written for George Bridgetower, an English violinist. Beethoven and Bridgetower gave the first performance in 1803.

Later Beethoven dedicated the piece to Rodolphe Kreutzer (shown left), a brilliant violinist from Paris, after hearing him play in Vienna.

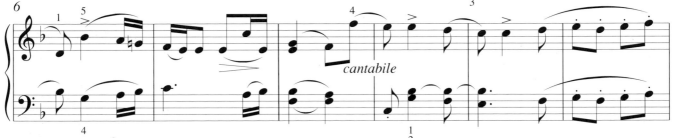

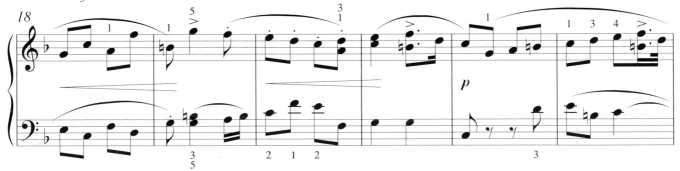

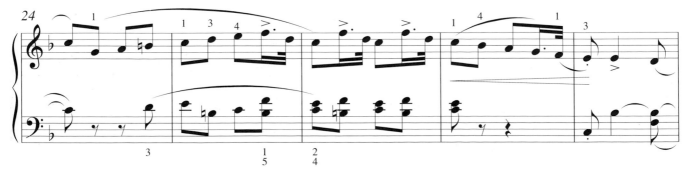

Although Kreutzer never played the piece, it became known as the Kreutzer Sonata. For more about nicknames given to Beethoven's pieces, see page 44.

Tolstoy, a Russian novelist, wrote a story called *Kreutzer-sonata*, based on a performance of this piece. This then inspired a quartet by the composer Janáček.

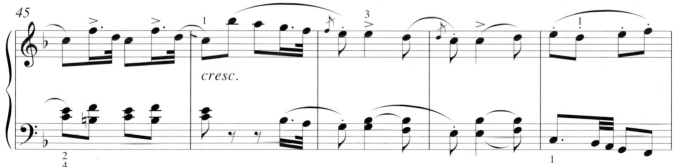

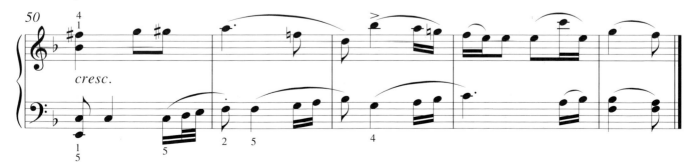

Variations on "God save the King"

In variations, the composer starts with a theme and then repeats it several times, each time slightly altered. There is more about variations on page 34.

This is the theme and two out of seven variations on the English tune "God save the King". When it was written, George III, shown on the left, was King of England.

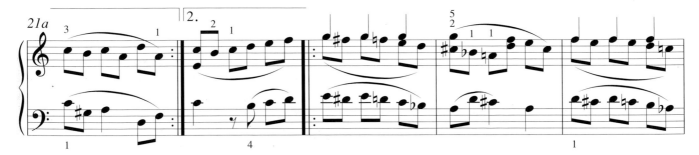

Outside Austria, Beethoven was most popular in England. He wrote many arrangements of British folk tunes and dances for a publisher in Scotland.

Beethoven planned several times to visit England, and wanted to give the first performance of his seventh symphony there. But none of the visits took place.

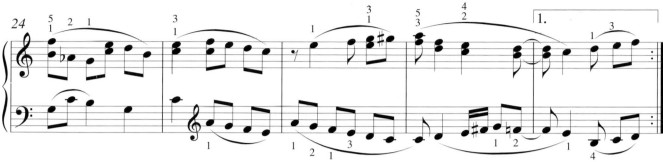

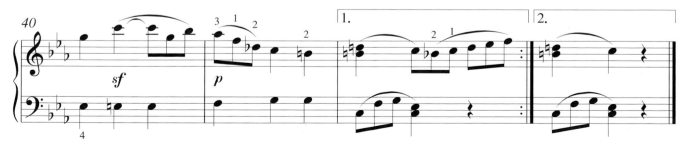

Eroica Symphony, op.55

The title of Beethoven's third symphony means "Heroic". He wrote it in 1803. Originally he dedicated it to Napoleon Bonaparte (see below).

This section of music, from the slow movement, is a funeral march. You can find out more about Beethoven's symphonies on page 35.

The Eroica Symphony was originally called "Bonaparte". This was in honor of Napoleon Bonaparte, a French general who defended the new French Republic after the Revolution. (For more about this, see page 15.) At first, Beethoven greatly admired Napoleon for his heroism and bravery. But he became disillusioned when Napoleon, ambitious for his own glory, decided to crown himself emperor in 1804. Horrified and angry, Beethoven tore the title page of his symphony in two.

Napoleon crowning himself, based on a contemporary sketch

Beethoven wrote this piece while living in Döbling (shown right), near Vienna. His house was by a stream, surrounded by fields and vineyards.

At the time, he was also working on his sixth symphony, the Pastoral Symphony. In this piece he expressed his delight in his natural surroundings.

When Beethoven received a copy of the score of the symphony from the publisher he scratched out the original title so hard that he went through the paper. You can see the scratched title page on the right. In the end he called it the "Heroic" symphony and

dedicated it to "the memory of a great man".

But in spite of this, Beethoven did retain some admiration for Napoleon. Even in 1824, long after Napoleon's defeat, he remembered him as a great and noble figure.

Razumovsky Quartet, op.59 no.2

This quartet was commissioned in 1806, along with two others, by Count Razumovsky. He was the Russian ambassador in Vienna, and a wealthy patron.

On Razumovsky's request, Beethoven included a Russian theme in two of the quartets. On the left you can see Beethoven playing to Razumovsky's family.

Allegretto (♩. = 69)

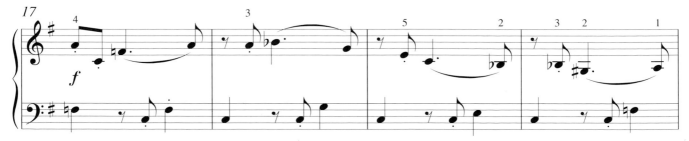

Count Razumovsky was one of Beethoven's strongest supporters for many years. He also sponsored a resident string quartet at his palace in Vienna.

Razumovsky lost much of his wealth when a fire destroyed a large part of his palace in 1814. By 1816, he could no longer afford to employ the quartet.

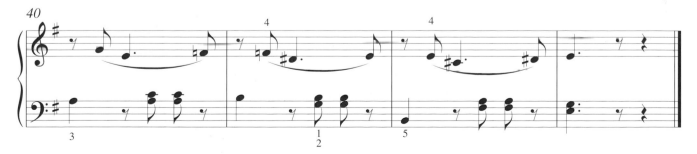

Variations

A variation movement

eethoven changed and developed many musical forms (ways of organizing pieces). One of the forms which he was very interested in was variations. In variations, there is a main tune (called the theme) which is repeated several times.

Beethoven composing

Each time the theme is repeated, it is slightly altered. The first piece Beethoven published was a set of variations, and he experimented with the form all his life. Almost half his pieces for instruments are sets of variations, or have movements which are sets of variations.

Beethoven worked out some of his variations in very simple ways (see box below), like previous composers had done. He would hide the notes of the theme among other notes, change the rhythm slightly, or write one of the variations in a minor key, instead of in the major. But although the theme is disguised and ornamented, it is still fairly easy to recognize.

In many of his variations, however, Beethoven was far more imaginative than any previous composer. He wanted to find out how much he could change the theme before it would stop being recognizable. He also tried to give an overall shape to his sets of variations, not leave them as small separate sections, all about the same length.

For example, in one piece, he made each variation start a third lower than the previous one, working his way through all the keys. In other sets, instead of

Many of Beethoven's string quartets contain variations.

adding notes to the theme, he took parts of it away, leaving a kind of skeleton. Only a rhythm pattern or accompaniment from the original theme might be left. Then he used this skeleton to compose a whole new section. He wrote his last set of variations after Anton Diabelli, a composer and publisher, asked 50 composers in Vienna to write a variation on one of his waltzes. Beethoven wrote a set of 33, which Diabelli published in 1823.

Anton Diabelli

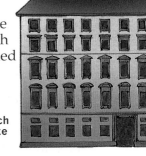
In this house where Beethoven lived, each set of windows is like a variation.

How variations work

These music examples show how Beethoven worked out variations on the theme of "God save the king". You can play the theme and two of the variations on pages 28-29.

The theme is in C major, and is mainly in quarter notes. The tune is easy to hear.

This variation is in the same key as the theme. The notes printed in red are the notes of the theme.

The notes are mostly eighth notes. The theme notes are hidden among ornamental notes (printed black).

In the third bar the theme notes start to come an eighth note later than you expect. This is called syncopation.

This variation is the fifth in the set. It is in a different key from the theme: C minor instead of C major.

There are three notes to each beat (triplets), more ornamental notes and more syncopation.

In other variations, the tune is hidden among sixteenth notes or disguised as a march with four beats in a bar.

Beethoven completed nine symphonies, and made sketches for a tenth. They are perhaps the most popular and important of all his pieces. They show how he changed and developed ideas about music.

In Beethoven's time, the symphony was a fairly recent invention. It had grown out of the section of orchestral music at the start of an opera, known as the sinfonia. Composers such as Mozart and Haydn expanded the sinfonia to a piece with four movements. The first and last movements were usually fast, and the second was slow. The third movement was usually a minuet (a kind of French dance).

The minuet was a slow, dignified dance.

The movements of a symphony were usually written in sonata form (there is more about this in the box on the right).

Beethoven changed both the overall size and length of the symphony, and the structure of its individual movements. Haydn, for example, tended to begin his symphonies with a

The Theater an der Wien, where Beethoven's fifth and sixth symphonies were first performed

movement lasting for about 200 bars. But the first movement of Beethoven's third symphony, the Eroica, is more than 500 bars long. At the time, this was the longest symphony movement ever written. Beethoven went on to write even longer ones.

In his sixth symphony, the Pastoral, Beethoven also expanded the total number of movements to five, and gave each one a descriptive title (for more about this, see pages 38-39). But his most ambitious symphony is his last, the ninth, known as the Choral Symphony.

Beethoven's dedication of his ninth symphony to the King of Prussia

The last movement of the Choral Symphony is Beethoven's longest. It is more than 900 bars long. In it, he uses not only a large orchestra, but a choir and solo singers as well.

To make very long movements stay interesting, Beethoven had to invent a new way of organizing them. He did this by turning sonata form into a kind of musical puzzle. This is explained in the box on the right. Instead of starting with clear themes, he simply gives hints of a tune at first. Most of the movement is a kind of search for the real theme. This theme is only finally put together at the end.

How Beethoven changed sonata form

Below, the top three diagrams show how composers such as Haydn and Mozart used sonata form. The bottom three diagrams show how Beethoven changed it.

 Haydn and Mozart usually began with clear themes, in different keys.

 These themes were then combined and varied in many different ways.

Finally the themes were repeated, but in the same key. The piece ended with a short section called a coda.

 Beethoven starts with hints of a simple, changing tune or rhythm.

He juggles with the hints in a search for the theme. This is a long section.

Finally, the hints come together, and the theme appears. The coda continues to emphasize this theme in new ways.

The Kärntnerthor theatre where the ninth symphony was first performed

Violin concerto, op.61

Beethoven composed this piece for a special concert put on to raise money for the violinist Franz Clement. Clement performed it at the concert.

Some experts think that Clement suggested this tune for the last movement. At the time, most people considered the concerto too difficult to play.

The conversation books

From 1818, Beethoven had to ask visitors to write down what they wanted to say in notebooks, because he could not hear them. Many of these conversation books have survived. Beethoven used them in rehearsals so the performers could communicate with him. Some of the entries refer to visits from other famous composers, such as Franz Liszt and Carl Maria von Weber, or are about their music. Beethoven also used the notebooks for writing down shopping lists and drafting letters.

Symphony no.5, op.67

Beethoven finished writing this symphony in 1808 and conducted the first perfomance in the same year. This music is from the second movement.

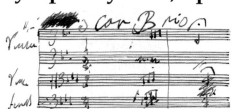

You can see the opening bars of the first movement on the left. Beethoven said the first four notes were inspired by the song of a bird called a yellowhammer.

Andante con moto ($\quad$ = 92)

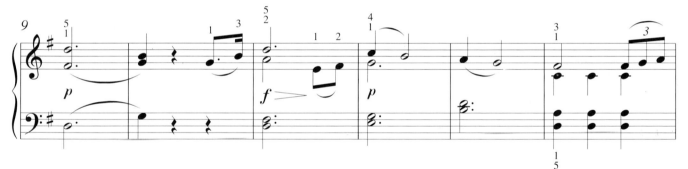

Pastoral Symphony, op.68

The Pastoral Symphony is Beethoven's sixth. He finished writing it while he was living at Heiligenstadt. In it he expressed his feelings about nature.

Sixième SINFONIE ~pastorale~

The piece has five movements (sections). The music on this page is from the first one. The music on the opposite page is from the fifth movement.

Allegro ma non troppo (♩ = 66)

[musical score]

Program music

Program music directly refers to, or depicts, real or imaginary events or situations. It can tell a story or paint a picture of a scene. Many composers, from the early eigteenth century to the present day, have written pieces of program music.

Experts often describe the Pastoral Symphony as an example of program music. Beethoven himself felt the music had more to do with feelings than descriptions. But despite this, he gave each movement a descriptive title, and in one section imitated the songs of

specific birds (see opposite). On the manuscript of the first movement, Beethoven wrote "Awakening of happy feelings on arrival in the country". He described the next two movements as a scene by a brook and a gathering of country folk. He called the fourth movement "Storm", and described the final movement (the music on the opposite page) as a "shepherd's song: happy and thankful feelings after the storm". The picture on the left is based on a 19th century illustration of Beethoven composing this piece.

Beethoven began to sketch this symphony before starting to work on his fifth, but in the end he finished the fifth a few months before it.

The fifth and sixth symphonies and the fourth piano concerto were first performed in one big concert. This was held in 1808, in the theatre shown on the left.

Allegretto (♩. = 60)

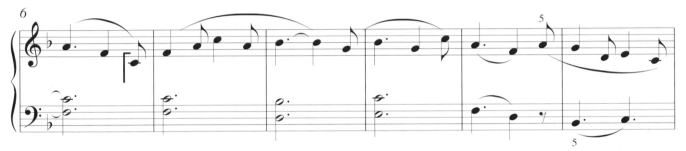

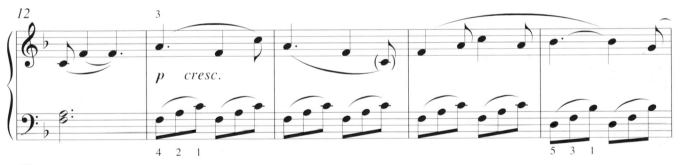

Birdsong

Beethoven included recognizable imitations of birdsong in the Pastoral Symphony. He wrote the songs down as music himself. He wrote the names of the birds he was imitating (a nightingale, quail and cuckoo) next to the notes in the score.

The section of Beethoven's manuscript showing the nightingale's song

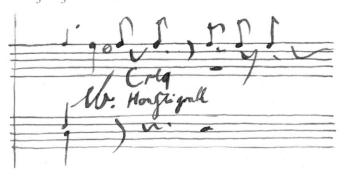

Für Elise

This piece is a bagatelle. The title means "For Elise", but nobody knows who this was. It was written for a woman called Therese Malfatti (shown right).

Beethoven asked her to marry him in 1810, but she refused. He gave her a private copy of this piece, which was not published until 1867.

Andante

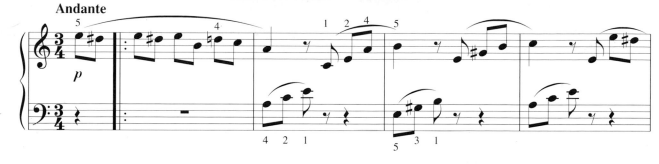

Harp Quartet, op.74

This piece is for a string quartet, which consists of two violins, a viola and a cello. There is more about string quartets at the bottom of the page.

It has become known as the Harp Quartet because in one section the cellist has to pluck the strings. This makes a sound a bit like a harp.

String quartets

The string quartet was first established as a serious kind of music by Beethoven's teacher, Haydn. Beethoven himself wrote sixteen string quartets. They are often regarded as his greatest pieces of chamber music and also some of the most important

and influential string quartets ever written. Many experts think that the five quartets Beethoven composed in the last two years of his life are his greatest. They are known as the late quartets. You can play part of one of them on page 59.

41

Beethoven's brother, Caspar Carl, signed a document while he was ill, naming Beethoven as the guardian of his nine year old son, Karl. He later realized that Beethoven wanted sole responsibility for the boy. But he wanted his wife Johanna to be a guardian as well. He wrote this in a new will which he made the day before he died.

Beethoven disliked Johanna and wanted her to have nothing to do with bringing up Karl. For five years he fought long, bitter legal battles against her. Eventually, in 1820, he won sole guardianship of Karl.

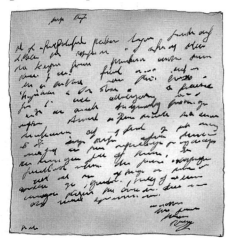

A letter written by Beethoven to his nephew, Karl

At this time, Beethoven began to worry about money. His legal battles over Karl were very expensive. He was earning less from public performances because his music was becoming less fashionable in Vienna. Until about 1817, he was also composing less, because his new method of writing music was difficult and time consuming.

Several of his patrons had died, including Lichnowsky, who died in March 1814. In order to raise money, Beethoven was frequently dishonest with his publishers (for more about this see page 22).

From 1817, Beethoven began to sketch parts of his ninth symphony and a huge religious choral piece, the Missa Solemnis.

Portrait of Beethoven composing the Missa Solemnis

In the six years it took him to finish composing the Missa Solemnis, Beethoven also wrote several other pieces, including four piano sonatas. One of these, known as the Hammerklavier, was the longest piano sonata he ever wrote. Unlike most other piano music of the time, the Hammerklavier was much too difficult for ordinary people to play. Many experts think that the music Beethoven wrote at around this time is his best.

Title page of Beethoven's Hammerklavier Sonata

Karl van Beethoven

Karl lived with Beethoven when he left school in 1823, acting as his secretary while continuing to study. But by 1826 he found his uncle's eccentric manner unbearable and tried to kill himself. Later he joined the army and married.

Karl van Beethoven

Sketches of Beethoven

Mödling, near Vienna, where Beethoven worked on the Hammerklavier Sonata and the Missa Solemnis

Deafness

Beethoven gradually became almost completely deaf. In 1822, he tried to conduct a choir and orchestra in rehearsals for a concert. He waved the baton wildly, unable to hear a note, and caused complete confusion. He was desperately upset. In 1824, in another concert of his music, he insisted on standing next to the conductor, turning the pages and beating the tempo. The conductor was forced to instruct the orchestra to ignore Beethoven. At the end of the concert Beethoven had to be turned around to see the audience's applause, which he could not hear.

Beethoven conducting

Beethoven standing by the conductor during a concert

Beethoven could only hear his piano if he hit the keys very hard. After 1822, it seems that he gave up playing to other people. He concentrated more and more on composing. He often changed where he lived, and usually moved out to one of the villages near Vienna during the summer.

In 1823, he completed the Missa Solemnis and a piece for piano called the Diabelli Variations. In 1824, he finished his ninth symphony and began to write a series of five string quartets. This was the first time he had concentrated so much on one type of piece.

A page from the manuscript of the last movement of the ninth symphony

His last illness

Beethoven was often ill, with fevers, liver diseases and other problems. In 1825, after a serious illness, his doctors prescribed a strict diet for him. When he recovered, Beethoven composed a "Sacred Song of Thanksgiving" as part of one of his string quartets, op.132.

In September 1826, Beethoven became ill again. He was staying with his brother, Nikolaus Johann, at his house in a village outside Vienna. After an argument with him at the beginning of December, he left for Vienna. He stayed overnight in a

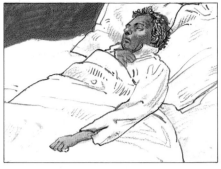

Beethoven on his death bed

cold, damp hotel, and developed a fever and bad cough.

For the next four months Beethoven's health got steadily worse. By March it was clear that he was going to die. He made his will on March 23, and died three days later.

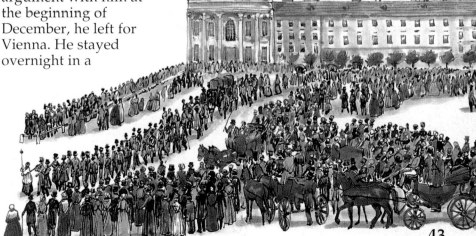

Beethoven's will

At least 10,000 people joined Beethoven's funeral procession. Despite his reputation for being bad-tempered and eccentric, his genius was widely recognized.

Beethoven's funeral procession

43

Archduke Trio, op.97

Beethoven wrote this piece in 1811. It is for a piano trio, which consists of a piano, a violin and a cello. Beethoven also wrote six other pieces for piano trio.

The piece got its name because it was dedicated to Archduke Rudolph of Austria (shown left), who was a pupil, friend and patron of Beethoven.

Nicknames

Many of Beethoven's works are known by nicknames. Some, such as the Eroica Symphony, the Pastoral Symphony, and the Appassionata Sonata were named by Beethoven himself. Others were named by Beethoven's contemporaries. For example, Rellstab, a critic, said that the first movement of one piano sonata reminded him of moonlight shining over a lake. It has been known as the Moonlight Sonata ever since. Several pieces were named after the person they were dedicated to, such as the Archduke Trio, the Razumovsky Quartets and the Kreutzer Sonata.

Other pieces were given their nicknames after Beethoven's death, for example the Ghost Trio (because of the ghostly slow movement), the "Rage over a lost penny" (because it sounds very angry) and the Harp Quartet (see page 41).

This 19th century picture was inspired by Beethoven's Moonlight Sonata.

Archduke Rudolph was one of the five Viennese noblemen who made a contract guaranteeing Beethoven a regular income (see page 25).

Beethoven dedicated several other pieces of music to Archduke Rudolph, including a piano concerto and a piano sonata (shown left).

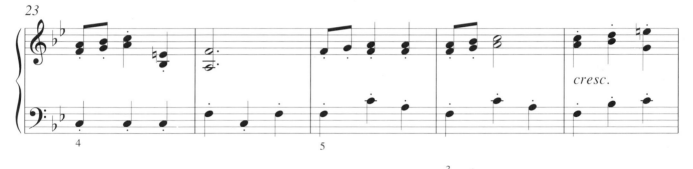

Houses

In the 40 years that Beethoven lived in Vienna, he changed where he lived more than 70 times. Each time he moved, he quickly discovered something about his new home that he did not like. For example, he complained that people living nearby were noisy, that he could be heard composing and talking, that the rooms faced the wrong way or that there was no view. As was usual at that time, Beethoven always lived in rented accommodation. He tried once to buy a house, but was unsuccessful.

Beethoven rarely took any time off, but like many Viennese people he often moved out of the city during the summer. He usually stayed in one of the villages near Vienna, such as Heiligenstadt, Mödling or Bad Teplitz (shown in the picture on the right), often in places recommended to him by his doctors.

Symphony no.7, op.92

Beethoven conducted the first performance of this symphony in 1813. The concert was held at the old university in Vienna (shown right).

The concert was a charity event in aid of wounded Austrian and Bavarian soldiers. It was so successful that it was repeated four days later.

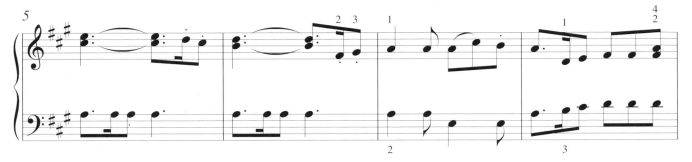

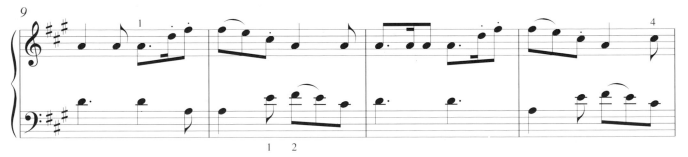

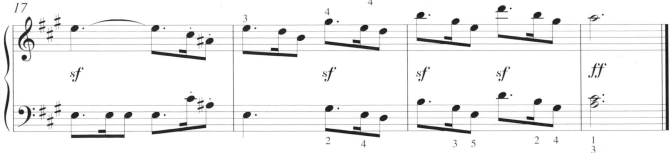

An die ferne Geliebte, op.98

This piece was the first song cycle ever written. A song cycle is a set of songs linked by their music and subject. This cycle contains six songs.

Beethoven wrote this piece in 1816. The title means "To the distant beloved". The picture on the left was on the title page of the original edition.

When Beethoven began his career as a pianist and composer, the piano was a recent invention, still being developed and improved. But it was already enormously popular, and Beethoven composed a great deal of music for it, including 32 sonatas and 5 concertos.

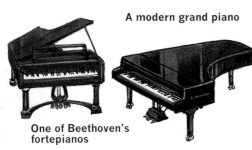

A modern grand piano

One of Beethoven's fortepianos

The pianos which Beethoven used are known as fortepianos. They were much quieter than modern pianos. This is because they were made entirely of wood, with light, loose strings. (A modern piano has an iron frame, and much heavier and tighter strings.) This means, for example, that when Beethoven's piano trios were first performed, the fortepiano player had to play much more loudly than a modern pianist would, just to be heard above the other instruments.

A piano trio using a fortepiano

The fortepiano also made a less smooth sound than a modern piano. This is because the hammers that struck the strings were covered in hard leather, not thick, soft felt.

On some fortepianos the sound could be altered in a variety of ways. The player conrolled the changes with foot pedals, or hand or knee levers. Two main ways invented to alter the sound are still used today. Felt blocks called dampers were rested on the strings to make the sound quieter, or held away from them to sustain the sound. Also, the hammers could be made to strike fewer strings (there were usually three for each note). This made the sound much quieter.

A fortepiano with several pedals for different effects

A "square" fortepiano

The notes on a fortepiano died away much more quickly than they do on a modern piano, even with a sustaining pedal. For example, in the first movement of the Moonlight Sonata Beethoven tells the player to hold down the sustaining pedal throughout. On a fortepiano, with the sustaining pedal down, every note could still be heard clearly. But on a modern piano, each note would last so long that the music would sound blurred and confused. A player today has to keep lifting the sustaining pedal and pressing it again.

Fortepianos also had fewer notes than a modern instrument.

Pedal marks in the Moonlight Sonata

Most pianos today have 88 notes, from a low A to a top C. Beethoven's first fortepiano had 63 notes, and his last one still only 78. Some experts think that parts of his music show that he "ran out" of notes at the top or the bottom of the piano keyboard. For example, a rising tune might suddenly jump down an octave when it reached the highest note on Beethoven's instrument. Sometimes he also made allowances for any player whose piano might have a smaller range than his, by suggesting an alternative note, usually the octave below or above.

This fortepiano has knee pedals just below the keyboard.

A piano maker's workshop

The orchestra

Until public concerts became very popular in the middle of the 18th century, orchestras contained different instruments according to where they played. A court orchestra in Austria in 1760, for example, probably did not include trombones, but church orchestras and Italian opera orchestras of the same time did. When audiences began to demand all the latest music, wherever it came from, orchestras had to be flexible and include different instruments.

Instruments in Beethoven's expanded orchestra

Contra-bassoon · Trombone · Piccolo · Clarinet

In his later symphonies, Beethoven introduced several instruments to the orchestra. These included the trombone, the piccolo (small flute) and the contrabassoon (large bassoon).

The groups of instruments brought together in the orchestra had developed separately. For example, from the 17th century, string players usually played in large groups, with several players to a part, and woodwind players in smaller bands. Brass players usually played alone. Horns were used mainly out of doors in hunting, and trumpets for fanfares or in the army.

A Russian wind band

These traditions influenced how Beethoven and other composers used instruments in the orchestra. For example, there are always more string players than woodwind and brass.

In Beethoven's time, each instrument still retained its individual character and distinct sound in the orchestra. Many, such as horns, were also limited to a fairly small range of notes or keys. But in the 30 years after Beethoven's death, instruments changed rapidly. They became much more flexible, and their sounds became smoother. This meant that they blended together in the orchestra.

An 18th century horn

The orchestra also quickly grew in size. This was because many larger concert halls and opera houses had been built to accomodate growing audiences. This meant the orchestra had to become louder to be heard.

Today, some small orchestras try to recreate the sound of Beethoven's orchestra. They use 18th century instruments, or copies of them. Each instrument sounds very distinct. The violins have gut, not metal, strings, making them much quieter than modern ones. The bassoons have a coarser sound, and the wooden flutes sound sharp and breathy.

The Singakademie, a large hall in Berlin

The timpani have calfskin heads and are played with wooden sticks, giving them a less distinct pitch than modern drums.

A modern orchestra using 18th century instruments

Timpani · Flutes · Violins · Bassoons

Symphony no.8, op.93

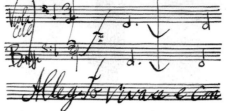

Beethoven wrote this symphony in 1812. The first movement was originally intended for a piano concerto. This music is from the last movement.

Unusually, Beethoven, did not dedicate this piece to anyone. At the time, he was angry with Lichnowsky, who had cut his financial support.

Beethoven's deafness

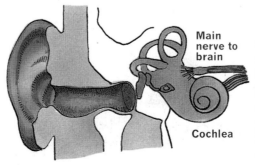

The type of deafness which Beethoven had is called nerve deafness. This means that the nerves in a part of the ear called the cochlea, which turn sounds into messages for the brain, are dead. At first Beethoven could not hear high sounds. Later he also heard continuous ringing and howling noises. Bedrich Smetana, a Czech composer, also had nerve deafness. In one of his string quartets, the first violin plays a very long, high note. This imitates the ringing sound both composers had in their ears.

At about this time, metronomes became widely available (see below). This symphony was the first one in which Beethoven included a metronome marking.

He wrote an article in a local paper praising the metronome. Later he published a list of metronome markings for all his previous symphonies as well.

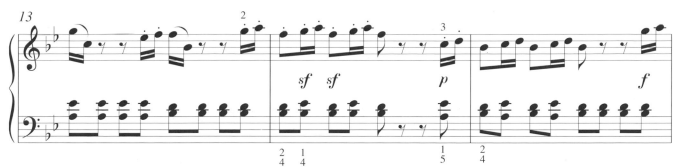

Maelzel's inventions

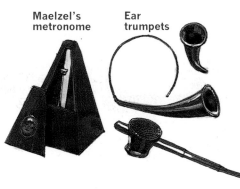

Maelzel's metronome   **Ear trumpets**

Maelzel was a German inventor who lived in Vienna. He was a friend of Beethoven and made the metronome which Beethoven used. Until recently, people thought Beethoven's metronome markings were too fast, making his music sound confused.

Experts now realize that on 18th century instruments, or copies of them, his music sounds clear and exciting played very fast.

Maelzel also made several ear trumpets for Beethoven, and a mechanical orchestra for which Beethoven wrote a piece.

Violin sonata, op.96

This is the last violin sonata that Beethoven wrote. It was first performed in Vienna on December 19, 1812, but was not published until 1816.

Beethoven dedicated the piece to Archduke Rudolph (see page 44). The Archduke gave the first performance with Pierre Rode, a French violinst.

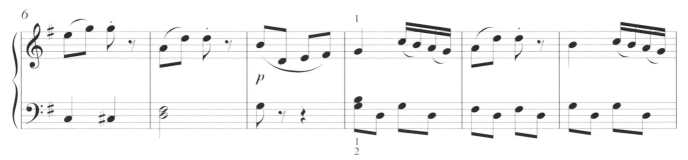

Sonatas

A sonata is a piece in several movements (usually three) for one or two instruments. Most sonatas are for piano alone, or piano and another instrument.

Beethoven composed more sonatas than any other kind of music, including 32 for solo piano. He performed many of his early piano sonatas himself, often adapting or improvising parts of them during a concert. In his later piano sonatas he exploited all the power and volume which many new, improved pianos were capable of. These sonatas are among his most personal and expressive music.

He also wrote ten sonatas for violin and piano, five for cello and piano and one for horn and piano. In these, instead of making the piano accompany the other instrument, he made both parts equally important and difficult. He was one of the first composers to do this.

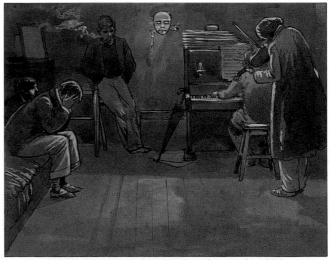

A performance of the Kreutzer Sonata in 1900

In 1815, Beethoven was made an honorary citizen of Vienna. This was to honor him for his fame and talent, and to encourage him to stay in Vienna.

Other distinctions awarded to him in his lifetime included membership of the Music Academy of Stockholm (see left) and the Academy of Amsterdam.

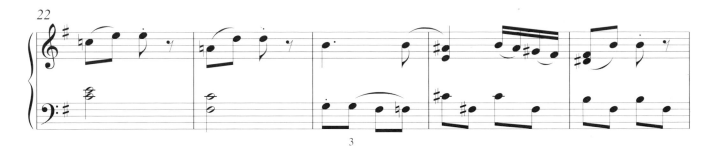

Beethoven's friends

Although Beethoven was often moody and temperamental, he had some very loyal friends. Both Prince Lichnowsky and Archduke Rudolph were close friends as well as patrons. When the Archduke and his family were forced to leave Vienna,

Beethoven wrote a sonata dedicated to him and called the movements "Farewell", "Absence" and "The Return".

Beethoven's greatest friends were the Breuning family. Stephan Breuning had been a childhood friend, and helped

Beethoven with the libretto of *Fidelio*. Stephan's wife also helped him to run his household. Beethoven was particularly fond of their son, Gerhard, whom he called Ariel or Pantsbutton. Gerhard wrote his recollections of Beethoven in 1874.

A silhouette of the Breuning family

Fidelio, op.72

Beethoven was very interested in music for the theatre. In 1803 he was appointed composer for the main theatre in Vienna (shown on the right).

Fidelio, first staged in 1815, is the only opera which Beethoven completed. The first version, *Leonore*, was a failure when it was performed in 1805.

The plot of *Fidelio*

The heroine of *Fidelio* is Leonore, wife of a Spanish nobleman called Florestan. Florestan has been unjustly imprisoned by a tyrannical governor called Pizarro. Leonore disguises herself as a man, and calls herself Fidelio. She becomes an assistant to Rocco, who is Pizarro's jailer. She is about to rescue Florestan and shoot Pizarro, when the King's Minister, Don Fernando (the just ruler), arrives to free the prisoners. The pictures on the right are based on 19th century illustrations of the plot of *Fidelio*.

Rocco realizes his daughter loves Fidelio.

Beethoven rewrote *Leonore* twice, tried libretti (words) by three poets, reworked many songs, and wrote four overtures. The final version was a huge success.

In *Fidelio*, Beethoven explored an idea he was very interested in, that of the just ruler. It was the first opera to have such a strong political message.

Pizarro tells Rocco to dig Florestan's grave.

The grave is finished.

Leonore prevents Florestan's murder.

Bagatelle, op.126 no.5

This piece is the fifth bagatelle in a set of six which Beethoven wrote in 1824. This was the same year that he finished writing his ninth symphony.

These later bagatelles, although they sound simple, are packed with new and brilliant musical ideas. They are among his most important compositions.

Quasi allegretto

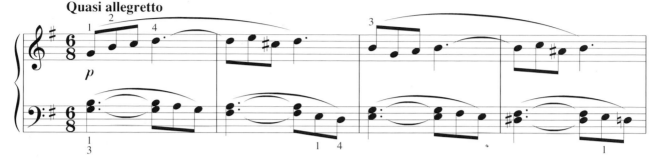

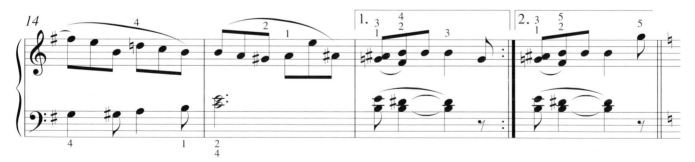

They work in a similar way to
his late quartets and sonatas,
using simple forms and musical
ideas to make very dense,
complicated pieces.

They are unlike his earlier, more
light-hearted bagatelles, such as
the one on page 21, which had
not been regarded as very
serious or important.

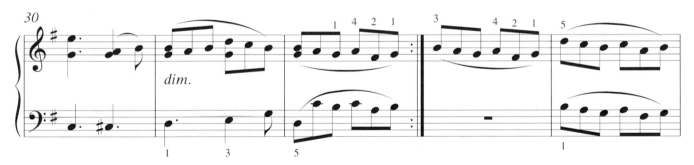

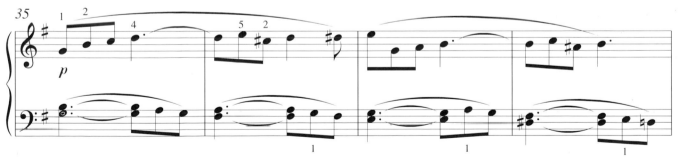

Symphony no.9, op.125

This symphony is often called the Choral Symphony. The last movement is a setting of a poem by Schiller, a famous German poet, for solo singers and chorus.

This was the last symphony which Beethoven completed. He dedicated it to the King of Prussia (see left). This music is from the third movement.

Adagio molto e cantabile

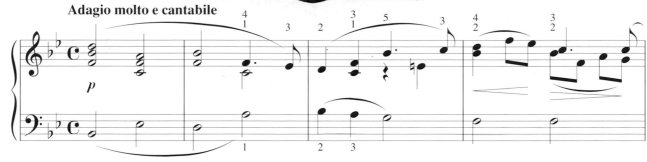

String quartet, op.130

Beethoven wrote this quartet in 1826 at his brother's house in Gneixendorf. It was performed in the hall shown here. This is the fourth of six movements.

Beethoven marked this music "Alla danza tedesca", which means "in the style of a German dance", a waltz. But it should be played slower than a dance.

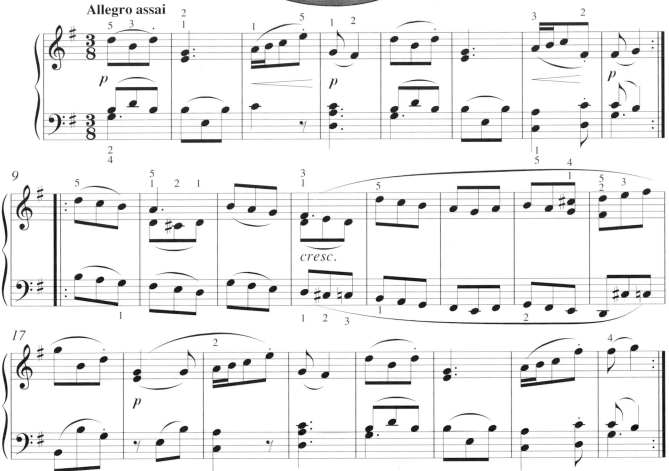

Beethoven today

The picture on the right shows the monument to Beethoven in Vienna. Today, Beethoven is regarded as a great and heroic composer. He has probably influenced the music written after his death more than any other composer. Because Beethoven's music is so rich and complex, almost all modern composers, whatever kinds of music they write, have found something in it which they admire. They have used ideas from Beethoven's pieces to help them develop their own very different styles.

Beethoven's music is performed regularly all over the world. His setting of "Ode to Joy" in his ninth symphony is seen as one of the greatest expressions of the ideals of freedom and equality. It was chosen as the anthem of the European Community, and was performed in a concert on Christmas Day 1989 celebrating the beginning of the destruction of the Berlin Wall. A recording of the symphony has also been sent into deep space, on board the spacecraft Voyager II, as part of a large collection of information about human beings.

Playing the pieces

On these two pages you will find explanations and hints to help you play the music in this book. In general, when you are learning a piece, you need to practice any difficult parts slowly at first, each hand separately, until you can play them. Then try them faster if you need to, and finally try playing both hands together. There are fingering suggestions in the music which you can try. But if you find these uncomfortable, or cannot reach all of the notes easily, try working out your own fingering instead.

Sonatina

Where the eighth notes are slurred in pairs, as in bars 2 and 3, separate the second eighth note slightly from the next note. Where there are no slurs, play the notes very lightly. Practice the left-hand eighth notes separately until they sound fluent. In bars 26 and 29, *sim.* tells you to continue phrasing the eighth notes in groups of four. Make sure they are quieter than the tune.

Octet, op.103

Practice both parts of this duet before you play it with a friend. Then agree on a speed to play, and count a few bars aloud together before you start. Listen to your friend's playing so you stay together. Do not play too loudly, or the repeated notes might sound heavy and plodding. Player A starts with the tune, but player B takes over in bar 9, so player A has to play more quietly. Both players have the tune from the middle of bar 17. In part A, practice playing the grace notes as clearly with your left hand as you do with your right. In bar 14, move your left-hand finger quickly from the G, because player B needs it an eighth note later.

Mollys Abschied, op.52 no.5

Adagio means "slow". Practice the piano part on your own, before you try playing with a friend. Play very quietly and gently, or you will drown out the solo instrument. The right-hand line is the same as the solo line most of the time, but the piano plays in thirds with the tune in bars 11-12, and echoes it in bars 16-17.

Sextet, op.81

The first four bars are a single phrase which goes from one hand to the other. Make sure it sounds like one continous line. The sign in bar 4 tells you to play the C quarter note with your left hand. From bar 32, watch out for the phrase marks and stress the first note of each bar slightly, so that the right-hand scales do not sound like exercises. Practice the big leaps in the right hand in bars 24-31. Play the piece fairly quickly, but no faster than you can manage these leaps.

Piano concerto no.1, op.15

Make sure your hands are precisely together when they have to play the same rhythm. If you are right handed, your left hand may lag a bit. Play lightly, to bring out the staccato notes. Practice the rhythm carefully in bars 30-33.

Ah! Perfido, op.65

Take care not to make the three-note chords sound too heavy, and practice the sixteenth note sections carefully. If you play this with a friend, it is a good idea to practice the top and bottom lines, as well as the accompaniment, so you know exactly how the melody fits in. Play slightly more strongly where the piano echoes the melody (such as bars 7 and19) or joins with it (for example, bars 15 and 20).

Quintet, op.16

The tune in this piece is played by a clarinet. To imitate this, try to make a soft sound, with a gentle accompaniment. Bring out the lower note of each pair of left-hand eighth notes slightly.

Bagatelle

Play this piece fairly lightly, taking care that the left-hand chords do not sound too loud. Stress the notes marked *sforzando* without hitting the keys too hard. Where there is a grace note just before a *sforzando* note, remember to play it quietly. Right after the *sforzando*, play quietly again to make a contrast.

Scherzo, op.9 no.2

Be sure which notes are staccato and which are slurred or legato. From bar 8, the left hand plays the tune. Bars 13-16 are fairly tricky, as all three lines are equally important. Practice this section carefully. Remember that the piece is for stringed instruments, so try to play smoothly.

Kreutzer Sonata, op.47

Stress the accented notes as if they were the first beat of the bar, but do not hit them too hard.

Variations on "God save the King"

In the theme (bars 1-14) do not make the chords too heavy. In the variations, emphasize slightly the notes from the tune (there is more about this on page 34). In bar 13 you have to play a triplet with your right hand and eighth notes with your left hand. Practice tapping this rhythm by saying the words "nice cup of tea". Tap your right hand to the words "nice", "cup" and "tea" and your left hand to "nice" and "of".

Eroica Symphony, op.55

Play the first two notes of this piece, and the top two notes of the chord at the beginning of bar 2, with your right hand. Play the grace notes very quickly, but not too loudly. Make sure the three-note chords do not sound too heavy.

Razumovsky Quartet, op.59 no.2

The rhythm in this piece is a bit tricky at first. Practice tapping your hands in this sequence: left, right, right, left, left, right. Except for bar 8, this is the rhythm up to bar 21. Then the rhythm is reversed: right, left, left, right, right, left. Play the right-hand fortissimo chords loudly and clearly, but do not hit the keys too hard.

Violin concerto, op.61

Keep the left-hand chords delicate. In the right hand, stress the notes with a *tenuto* line. Play them firmly, but without accents.

Symphony no.5, op.67

Follow the dynamic marks very carefully. For example, from the last beat of bar 8 there is an echo of the previous phrase, then a louder repeat with extra notes added. At the end, a short phrase is repeated, first as an echo, then loudly.

Pastoral Symphony, op.68

In the first movement, take care to make the right-hand thirds light. The fifth movement begins with a four bar introduction. You could slow down very slightly at the end of bar 4 to emphasize the beginning of the main tune. *Dolce* means "sweet". Play the tune with a soft, singing tone, with a very gentle accompaniment.

Für Elise

Count in steady quarter note beats throughout this piece. Take care not to get lost, for example in bars 14-15. Do not play too slowly, and make the eighth notes sound flowing.

Harp Quartet, op.74

Make sure you play the left hand slightly more quietly than the tune. Practice the right hand in bars 8-11. Your thumb moves down in semitones.

Archduke Trio, op.97

The tune starts in the left hand, but goes into the right hand at bar 5. After bar 9 the left hand takes over again. Play the right-hand thirds lightly,

remembering the staccatos. Stress the *sforzando* notes in bars 12 and 28, then play quietly again.

Symphony no.7, op.92

The dotted rhythm switches from left to right every half bar at the beginning. Practice this so it sounds smooth and you can hear the melody.

An die ferne Geliebte

Lento means "slow". Play about 60 beats a minute, or slightly less, but do not let the music sound plodding. If you play this with a friend, listen very carefully to each other where you do not both play on the first beat of the bar. Do not let the piano drown the solo line, especially in bars 13 and 17, where it plays a higher note.

Symphony no.8, op.93

The repeated two-note chords should sound very gentle. The left hand takes over the tune in bars 3-4 and 7. Practice the octave jumps in the left hand in bars 18-19.

Violin sonata, op.96

Play the accompaniment smoothly and gently, but take care that the notes do not become blurred. Watch out for the staccato notes in the right hand at the end of each phrase.

Fidelio, op.72

Where the rocking eighth notes cross over into the right hand at bar 14, try to make them sound like a continuous line. They should always be a background to the tune. When the soloist is holding long notes, play the eighth notes more quietly, so they do not sound monotonous.

Bagatelle, op.126 no.5

Count very carefully in this piece, or play it with a metronome, or you may get lost. There are continuous eighth notes alternating between the hands, with syncopated and off-beat notes.

Symphony no.9, op.125

Molto adagio e cantabile means "very slow and in a singing style". Bring out the top note in the right-hand chords, as this is the melody. Stress the first right-hand chord in bars 7, 8, 9 and 10 slightly, then play more quietly. Watch out for all the dynamic markings.

String quartet, op.130

Practice the big leaps in the left hand in bars 16 and 17. Make sure you strike the two-note chords in the right hand evenly in bars 2, 6, 18 and 22.

Important dates in Beethoven's life

This chart lists the dates of some of Beethoven's most important compositions, as well as other events that took place during his lifetime.

1770   Beethoven born
William Wordsworth (poet) born
Friedrich Hölderlin (poet) born
Nicholas-Joseph Cugnot invents steam car
1772   Friederich von Schiller (poet) born
1773   Death of Ahmed Shah (founder of modern Afghanistan)
"Boston Tea Party": American sailors protesting against the Tea Act pour tea from English ships into the sea off Boston, Massachusetts
1774   Beethoven starts learning music
1776   American Declaration of Independence from Britain
1778   Beethoven's first public performance
Death of Voltaire (writer)
1779   Beethoven starts studying with Neefe
1781   Beethoven leaves school
George Stephenson (inventor of first successful steam engine) born
1782   Beethoven has his first piece published
1783   Montgolfier brothers invent hot air balloon
1784   Diderot (philosopher) dies
1787   Beethoven visits Vienna to play to Mozart
1789   French Revolution begins
1792   Beethoven begins studies with Haydn
Beethoven's father dies
William Murdock invents gas lighting
Charles Babbage (inventor of a calculating machine which was forerunner of the computer) born
1795   Beethoven's first public performance in Vienna, as soloist in the first piano concerto
1796   Composes *Ah! Perfido* and Quintet op.16
Edward Jenner discovers vaccination against the disease smallpox
1798   Beethoven starts to use sketchbooks
1800   Alessandro Volta invents the battery
1801   Beethoven first mentions hearing problems in a letter to Wegeler, a friend and physician
1802   Writes Heiligenstadt Testament
Composes Bagatelles op.33
1803   Moves into the Theater an der Wien
Composes Kreutzer Sonata
Erard, Parisian piano makers, send Beethoven a new, larger piano as a gift
Purchase of Louisiana from France, the largest land sale ever
Hector Berlioz (composer) born
1804   Napoleon proclaims himself Emperor; Beethoven tears up Eroica title page
Immanuel Kant (philosopher) dies
1805   Beethoven completes *Leonore*

Razumovsky commissions three string quartets from Beethoven
Battle of Trafalgar
1806   Beethoven's nephew, Karl, born
Beethoven quarrels with Lichnowsky
1807   Slave trade abolished in British Empire
1808   A serious infection nearly causes the loss of one of Beethoven's fingers
Composes Pastoral Symphony
1809   Contract guarantees Beethoven a salary
French capture Vienna; Beethoven hides in his brother's cellar to avoid the noise
Haydn dies
Charles Darwin (naturalist) born
Louis Braille (inventor of braille) born
Nikolai Gogol (novelist) born
1810   *Für Elise* presented to Therese Malfatti
1812   Completes seventh and eighth symphonies
Napoleon forced to retreat from Moscow in depth of winter, losing about 400,000 men
Beethoven writes to his "Immortal Beloved"
Charles Dickens (novelist) born
1813   Maelzel's metronome first advertised
Giuseppe Verdi (composer) born
Richard Wagner (composer) born
1814   Beethoven's last public performances
First performance of *Fidelio*
Count Razumovsky's palace destroyed by fire
1815   Brother Carl dies; battle over Karl begins
Battle of Waterloo; Napoleon defeated
Congress of Vienna to settle European states
1816   Composes *An die ferne Geliebte*
1817   Asks piano maker Streicher to make the loudest piano possible, to help him hear
1818   First uses conversation books
Karl runs away to his mother; Beethoven uses the police to get him back
1819   Unsuccessfully tries to buy a house
1820   Finally awarded guardianship of Karl
1822   Meets the Italian opera compser Rossini; Beethoven's deafness and the language barrier make the meeeting difficult
Liberia established by freed American slaves
1824   Completes ninth symphony
1825   World's first public railway opens in England, between Stockton and Darlington
1826   Karl tries to commit suicide
Beethoven composes his final string quartet
The second and third US presidents, John Adams and Thomas Jefferson, die on July 4, 50th anniversary of the signing of the Declaration of Independence
1827   Beethoven speaks his last words: "Pity, pity, too late."
Dies on March 26, reportedly during a storm
William Blake (poet) dies

Glossary

This list explains Italian terms used in this book, as well as other unfamiliar words. If a word appears in **bold** type within an entry, that word has its own separate entry in the list.

Adagio   Slow.

Allegretto   A little slower than Allegro.

Allegro   Fast, lively.

Andante   At a walking pace .

Aria   An operatic song.

Assai   Very. **Allegro** assai means "very fast".

Bagatelle   A short light piece. The word is French for "a trifle". It was first used in music by the French composer, Couperin. Beethoven's later bagatelles, however, are more serious.

Cantata   A piece for choir and orchestra. The word originally meant "sung", whereas "sonata" meant "sounded"(played).

Cantabile   In a singing style. In piano music this normally means "play **legato**".

Chamber music   Music for small groups of players (up to about eight), each playing a separate line of music.

Coda   The end part of a musical **form** (the word means "tail" in Italian). Beethoven made the coda an important section in many of his pieces.

Concerto   A piece written for orchestra and at least one **soloist**.

Dolce   Sweet.

Duet   A piece for two performers, with or without accompaniment.

Form   The structure of a piece; the way the music is organized.

Legato   Smoothly joined, with no break between the notes, or any particular emphasis.

Lento   Slow.

Libretto   The words of an opera or other large sung piece. The libretto is usually written first. One libretto may be used by several composers.

Lied (plural **lieder**)   A German song-style, which many experts say Beethoven invented. In the 19th century, many German and Austrian composers wrote lieder.

Minuet   An elegant French dance which has three beats to the bar. The word is also used for a piece which is in the style of a minuet. Before Beethoven's time, minuets were popular for one **movement** of a **sonata** or **symphony**.

Moderato   At a moderate speed.

Molto   Much, very. **Adagio** molto is very slow.

Moto   Movement, motion. **Andante** con moto means "with more motion than **Andante**".

Movement   An individual section of a larger piece, such as a **symphony** or **sonata**.

Octet   A group of eight instruments, or a piece of **chamber music** for eight players.

Poco   Little, somewhat. Poco allegretto means "a little slower than **Allegretto**".

Programme music   Music that tells a story or describes something.

Quasi   Almost, like. Quasi **Allegretto** means "in the style of an **Allegretto**".

Rondo   A musical **form** in which the **theme** reappears a number of times, with contrasting sections in between. Experts often give letter names to the different sections of a piece so they can describe its structure. They usually call the **theme** of a rondo A, with other letters for the contrasting sections. The structure of a rondo is often ABACA or ABACADA.

Scherzando   Jokingly, playfully.

Scherzo   Italian word meaning "joke". In Beethoven's music, a scherzo is a fast **movement** in a **sonata** or **symphony** with one main beat in the bar. Beethoven used the scherzo in place of the **minuet** used by earlier composers.

Sextet   A group of six instruments or a piece of **chamber music** for six players.

Sforzando   A strong accent.

Soloist   The performer in a **concerto** who plays the melody, accompanied by the orchestra. Also used for a performer playing or singing alone.

Sonata   A piece with more than one **movement**, usually three, for one or two instruments.

Sonatina   A short, simple, often light-hearted **sonata** (the word means "small sonata").

Song cycle   A set of songs that are linked, either by their subject or by a musical idea, for example a melody. Experts think Beethoven's *An die ferne Geliebte* was the first song cycle.

Staccato   Detached. A staccato note is usually shown by a dot above or below the note head.

String quartet   A group of two violins, one viola and one cello, or a piece of **chamber music** for that combination of instruments.

Symphony   A piece for orchestra usually consisting of three or four movements.

Tenuto   Held. A tenuto note should be held for its full length, giving it a special emphasis. It is usually indicated by a short line above or below the note head.

Tempo   The speed at which a piece is played.

Theme   The musical term for a tune or melody. The word is particularly used for discussing the **form** of a piece.

Troppo   Too much. **Allegro** ma non troppo means "fast, but not too fast".

Vivace   Lively, but not necessarily very fast.

Waltz   A type of dance popular in the nineteenth century, especially in Vienna. Waltzes have three beats to the bar, but are usually faster than a **minuet**.

Index

accompaniment, 14
Ah! Perfido, 25
Albrechtsberger, Johann Georg, 5
Amsterdam, 53
Appassionata Sonata, 44
Archduke Trio, 44
Artaria, Domenico, 22
Artaria & Co., 22
Augarten (Vienna), 14

Bach, Johann Sebastian, 14
Bad Teplitz, 45
bagatelle, 21, 56-57
bassoon, 49
Bastille, 15
Beethoven, Caspar Carl van, 4, 25, 42
Beethoven, Johanna van, 42
Beethoven, Johann van, 4
Beethoven, Karl van, 25, 42
Beethoven, Ludwig van (grandfather), 4
Beethoven, Maria Magdalena van, 4
Beethoven, Nikolaus Johann van, 4, 43, 59
Berlin, 49
Berlin Wall, 59
birdsong, 39
Bonaparte, Napoleon, 15, 30-31
Bonn, 4-5, 8
brass instruments, 49
Brentano, Antonie, 25
Breuning, Gerhard, 53
Breuning, Stephan, 53
Bridgetower, George, 26
Browne-Camus, Count, 23

chamber music, 12-13, 41
Choral Symphony, 35, 58
clarinet, 49
Clary, Josephine von, 19
Clement, Franz, 36
cochlea, 50
concerto, 16-17
concerts, 14, 49
contrabassoon, 49
conversation books, 36
Cologne, Elector of, 4
copyright, 22

deafness, 43, 50-51
Diabelli, Anton, 34
Diabelli Variations, 34, 43
Döbling, 31
Don Fernando, 54
Dressler Variations, 4

Egmont, 14
England, 29
Eroica Symphony, 14, 24, 30-31, 35, 44
European Community, 59

Fidelio, 14, 53, 54-55
Florestan, 54
flute, 49
folk songs, 29
fortepiano, 48
Franz, Maximilian, 9
French Revolution, 15, 30

George III, 28
Ghost Trio, 44
Glorious Moment, The, 15
Gneixendorf, 59
Graf, Conrad, 25
Grätz Castle, 25

Hammerklavier Sonata, 14, 42
Harp Quartet, 44
Haydn, Joseph, 5, 14, 16, 24, 35, 41
Heiligenstadt, 24, 38, 45
Heiligenstadt Testament, 24
horn, 13, 49
houses, 45

"Immortal Beloved", 25

Janácek, Leos, 27

Keglevics, Babette, 16
Kreutzer, Rodolphe, 26
Kreutzer Sonata, 26-27, 44

Leonore, 54-55
libretto, 19, 53, 55
Lichnowsky, Prince, 5, 25, 42, 50, 53
lieder, 10-11
Liszt, Franz, 36
Lobkowitz, Prince, 24

Maelzel, Johann Nepomuk, 51
Malfatti, Therese, 40
Metastasio, Pietro, 19
metronome, 7, 51
Missa Solemnis, 42-43
Mödling, 42, 45
Moonlight Sonata, 44, 48
Mozart, Wolfgang Amadeus, 4, 14, 16, 20, 24-25, 35

Napoleon, *see* Bonaparte
Neefe, Christian Gottlob, 4-5
nicknames, 44

Ode to Joy, 59
opus, 3
orchestra, 49
overture, 55

Pastoral Symphony, 14, 31, 35, 38-39, 44
Pathétique Sonata, 5

pianos, 25, 48
sonatas, 52
piccolo, 49
Pizarro, 54
program music, 38
publishing, 5, 22

"Rage over a lost penny", 44
Razumovsky, Count, 32-33
Razumovsky Quartets, 32, 44
Rellstab, Ludwig, 44
Rocco, 54
Rode, Pierre, 52
Romanticism, 14
rondo, 17
Rudolph, Archduke of Austria, 44-45, 52, 53

"Sacred Song of Thanksgiving" (op.132), 43
Salieri, Antonio, 5
Schenk, Johann, 5
scherzo, 22
Schiller, Friedrich von, 58
Schubert, Franz, 10
Scotland, 29
sinfonia, 35
Singakademie (Berlin), 49
sketchbooks, 10-11
Smetana, Bedrich, 50
sonata, 52
sonata form, 35
sonatina, 6
song cycle, 47
songs, 10
Stockholm, 53
string instruments, 49
string quartets, 41
symphonies, 35, 49
Swieten, Baron van, 5

theme, 34, 35
timpani, 49
Tolstoy, Leo, 27
trombone, 49

variations, 28-29, 34
Vienna, 4-5, 8, 13, 24, 45
university, 46
violin, 49, 52
Voyager II, 59

watermarks, 23
Weber, Carl Maria von, 36
Wellington, Duke of, 15
Wellington's Victory, 15
woodwind instruments, 49

yellowhammer, 37